BATTLE OF THE CHORES
Junior Discovers Debt

by Dave Ramsey

Collect all of the *Junior's Adventures* books!

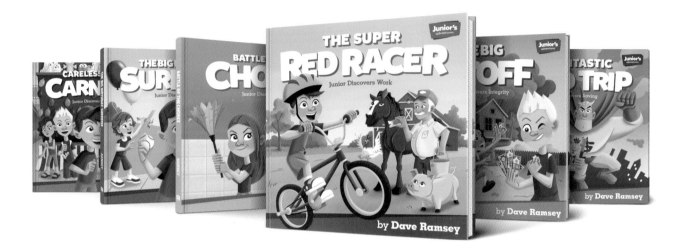

Battle of the Chores: Junior Discovers Debt
© 2015 Lampo Licensing, LLC
Published by Ramsey Press, The Lampo Group, Inc.
Brentwood, TN 37027

All rights reserved. No portion of this book may be reproduced, stored in a retrieval system, or transmitted in any form or by any means—electronic, mechanical, photocopy, recording, scanning, or other—except for brief quotations in critical reviews or articles, without the prior written permission of the publisher.

For more information on Dave Ramsey, visit daveramsey.com or call 888.227.3223.

Editors: Amy Parker, Jen Gingerich
Project Management: Preston Cannon, Bryan Amerine and Mallory Darcy
Illustrations: Greg Hardin, John Trent and Kenny Yamada
Art Direction: Luke LeFevre, Brad Dennison and Chris Carrico

DEDICATION

To award-winning illustrator Marshall Ramsey—my cousin and good friend. Thank you for working with us for more than a decade to bring Junior to life as the original illustrator. You are kind of Junior's "drawing father," and so you've helped us teach a whole generation of children about working, saving, spending, giving, debt, and integrity, and tens of thousands of families thank you.

And to Aunt Virginia and Uncle Dave—who I was named after. You've always exemplified the classic Ramsey way to live: work hard, spend wisely, and stay out of debt. It's an honor to be "the other Dave Ramsey" in our family.

—Dave

"Tomorrow's Saturday!" Junior popped a crouton into his mouth.
"A new *Dollar Bill's Adventures* DVD is coming out!"

"And we're going to the toy store. Right, Mom?" Rachel asked.
"I have enough saved for a new Sally Sweetheart doll!"

"Oh right, the toy store!" Junior looked over at the chore chart.
"Uhh, is that really all I did this week?"

The next morning after breakfast, Dad and Rachel counted up her chores for the week. She had earned her usual five dollars.

Dad looked at Junior's chores and raised an eyebrow. "So, Junior, what's that? A dollar fifty?"

"Um, yes."

"So, maybe you should step up the chores a bit next week?"

"Yes, sir."

Junior ran up to his room and grabbed his envelopes.
He put two quarters into the Give envelope
and opened the Save.

"Wow," he said, not impressed. "Five fifty."
He put the five fifty he had saved into
his Spend envelope and added the
dollar bill he earned this week.

"You ready, Junior?" Rachel asked, sticking her head into his room. "Mom's waiting."

"I'm coming." Junior put his Spend envelope in his back pocket and followed Rachel down the stairs.

"This is it!" Junior flipped over the new *Dollar Bill's Adventures* DVD to look at the price. "Ten dollars! I'm going to have to wait another whole week!"

He looked up to see Rachel coming around the corner with a new doll. "Look, Junior! Isn't she so cute?" Rachel gushed. "And I'll even have seven dollars left over!"

Just then, Junior had a **great** idea. . . .

On Monday after school, Junior finally had a chance to sit down with his new DVD, when Rachel came into the living room.

"Hey, Junior," Rachel said, "my room needs picked up."

"So?" Junior replied, still focused on the plastic wrapping.

"Sooo," Rachel sang, "you have to clean it for me. Remember?"

Junior dropped the DVD. "Right." He had promised to do Rachel's chores for a whole week to pay back the five dollars he had borrowed.

On Tuesday, Junior ran in the house, checked Rachel's room, and sat down with his DVD.

"Junior, did you see all of those toys in the backyard?"

"No."

"Well, I did. And you have to pick them up."

"Okay, okay. . . ." he mumbled all the way to the back door.

On Wednesday, Junior straightened Rachel's room, checked the backyard, and sat down with his DVD.

"Hey Junior, your turn to do the dishwasher," Rachel called.

"*Every* night is my turn to do the dishwasher," Junior whined.

"Just until you pay me back!" Rachel reminded him.

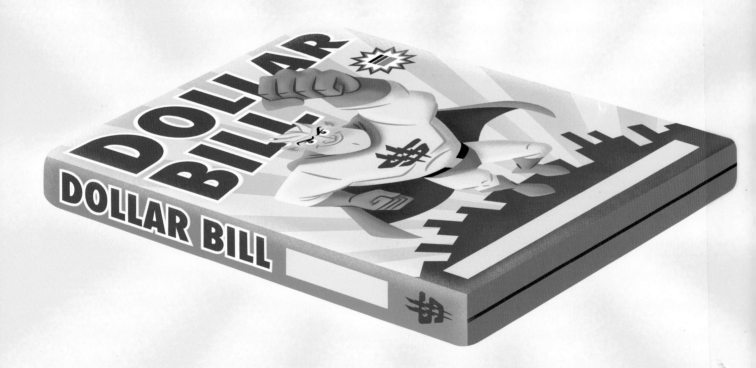

Junior left his DVD on the coffee table and sulked into the kitchen.

On Thursday, Rachel appeared out of nowhere.

"Thursday night!" she announced. "Our night to cook."

"Yeah," Junior remembered, "which means *my* night to cook."

He went into the kitchen, preheated the oven, mixed up a salad, very carefully put the pizza into the oven, set the table, and poured the drinks.

"Dinner's ready," he called and plopped into his chair.

"Don't forget to load the dishwasher,"
Rachel whispered when everyone was finished.

On Friday, Junior came home, did all of the chores, and went straight to bed. He didn't even think about the DVD still sitting unwrapped on the coffee table.

"Junior . . ." Mom walked slowly into his room and sat on the edge of his bed. "Are you feeling all right, honey?"

"Yes ma'am," Junior yawned. "I'm just a little tired."

Mom sighed. "Okay, snuggle in." She kissed his forehead. "And get some rest."

On Saturday, Junior
was scrubbing the
bathroom when Mom
walked by.

She did a double take.
"Junior, isn't it Rachel's turn
to clean the bathroom?"

"Uhh, yes," he answered,
searching for an explanation.
Then he decided to just tell
the truth.

"See, I didn't have enough money for the new Dollar Bill DVD . . ." he began.

About that time, Rachel poked her head in the door. "It was *his* idea," she explained. "And he promised to do all my chores to pay me back."

"I see." Mom leaned against the bathroom counter and looked at them both.

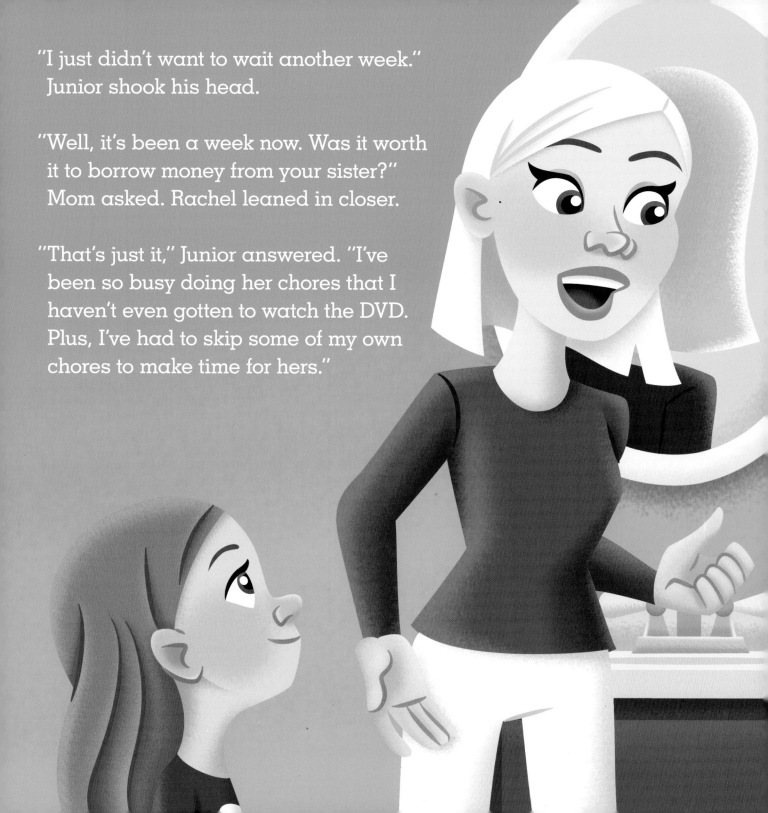

"I just didn't want to wait another week."
Junior shook his head.

"Well, it's been a week now. Was it worth
it to borrow money from your sister?"
Mom asked. Rachel leaned in closer.

"That's just it," Junior answered. "I've
been so busy doing her chores that I
haven't even gotten to watch the DVD.
Plus, I've had to skip some of my own
chores to make time for hers."

"When you go into debt, it kind of messes everything up. It not only changed the relationship between you and Rachel because you owed her money, but you're also right back where you started, huh?" Mom asked.

"Worse." Junior admitted. "I made *less* money of my own this week."

"I'm sorry, Junior." Rachel picked up the window cleaner and sprayed th mirror.

"You were just trying to help," Junior answered. "I really should've waited and earned my own money."

Rachel laughed and threw a paper towel at Junior. "Well, I won't ever loan you money again."

"Hey! Don't you worry." Junior threw it back at her, missing completely. "I won't ever ask to borrow money again."

That night, Junior and Rachel sat down and finall
watched the *Dollar Bill's Adventures* DVD.

And the next week, Junior was more than happy to do his—
and only his—chores.